Hado Bear's Secret

Written by Kathleen Quigley Caputo

Illustrated by Melanie Hall

"Hado" is pronounced "Hah-doe"

Illustrations and cover art by Melanie Hall
Cover and book interior design by Pilla Creative Marketing

Hado Bear is a trademark of Kathleen Caputo

Publisher's Cataloging-in-Publication
(Provided by Quality Books, Inc.)

Caputo, Kathleen Quigley, author.
    Hado Bear's Secret / written by Kathleen Quigley
Caputo; illustrated by Melanie Hall.
      pages cm
      SUMMARY: Hado Bear sits in the store wondering why no
one wants him. Then he is gifted to Janine who thinks no
one at school likes her. When Hado Bear reveals his
secret, they both discover they are perfect just the way
they are, and how positive thoughts attract good experiences.
      LCCN 2017906671
      ISBN 978-0-9988906-0-9

      1. Teddy bears–Juvenile fiction. 2. Loneliness–
Juvenile fiction. 3. Self-acceptance–Juvenile fiction.
[1. Teddy bears–Fiction. 2. Loneliness–Fiction.
3. Self-acceptance–Fiction.]   I. Hall, Melanie W.,
illustrator. II. Title.

PZ7.1.C3695Had 2017   [E]
             QBI17-800

Published by Hado Bear, Inc.
1001 2nd Avenue
Unit #149
New Hyde Park, NY 11040 - 9998

Author's Dedication

My parents, Marcia and Tom Quigley for their unconditional love.

All my family and friends who have encouraged me to live my passion of empowering children to have a happy and healthy life.

Ministers, Practitioners and Members of the Centers For Spiritual Living.

Special Thanks to the Following Friends Who Helped to Make this Book Possible

Cathy Gins, who knew Hado Bear was meant to be mine even before I realized it.

Tony Busse, for his vision, inspiration and business advice.

Lori Antonacci, for her marketing and publishing expertise.

Melanie Hall, for her contributions far beyond her beautiful illustrations.

Illustrator's Dedication

To Cathy Gins

Hado Bear's Secret

Written by Kathleen Quigley Caputo

Illustrated by Melanie Hall

"Hado" is pronounced "Hah-doe"

"Everyone will see you here," the storekeeper said as she placed the stuffed polar bear by the door of the gift shop.

"Oh, my, how exciting!" the bear said as the storekeeper walked away. The storekeeper turned around.

"Who said that?" she asked, puzzled. No one was in the shop. The storekeeper looked at the bear. The bear looked back at her innocently.

All that day, and the next day, too, the bear watched people strolling by and waited for someone to buy him. The bear tried to look charming and pleasant. Many people came into the shop and looked at him but no one bought him.

A little girl picked him up and hugged him asking, "Mom, can I have this bear?"

The bear held his breath, but the mother answered, "No, we don't have time now. Let's go!"

The child put him down, and the bear said sadly, "Bye!"

Surprised, the girl looked at him with wide eyes as her mother came to take her hand and they left the shop.

The day after, a little boy came in, looked at the bear, but chose the little brown dog. The following day, a little girl chose the red monkey and the gray and white striped cat for her birthday presents.

"Why doesn't anyone buy me?" the bear wondered. "Am I too big? Is my fur the wrong color? Maybe I need to be a dog or a cat. What do I have to do to have someone love me and take me home?"

Later that day, the bear saw two ladies walk by the shop. One of the ladies pointed to the bear. "Donna, wouldn't that adorable bear be a good present for your niece, Janine? Didn't you tell me that she is staying with you?"

Donna looked at the bear. Her eyes lit up. "Oh, Marie, he's so cute, I love him! There's something special about this bear that I can't explain. He would be a great present for Janine."

The bear's heart filled with joy as Donna paid the storekeeper and carried him away. She said goodbye to Marie and drove home with the bear beside her.

GIFT
SHOP
⟵
OPEN

The bear gazed out of the car window at the green trees and blue sky. He thought, "I am going home to be with my new family! I can't wait! But when should I tell my secret? Now?

"No, I'll wait until we get there."

As Donna walked through her front door with the bear, Janine and Uncle Bill rushed to hug her. Janine looked at the bear in her aunt's arms. "He's yours, Janine!" Donna told her.

Janine grabbed the bear and hugged him tightly. "Aunt Donna, he's the best present ever, thank you!" exclaimed Janine.

"This is the happiest day of my life," thought the bear.

"What will you name him, Janine?" asked Uncle Bill.

Janine thought long and hard. Everyone waited expectantly. "I've got it! Aunt Donna, do you remember telling me about 'Hado'? You said our lives are all made out of something that we cannot see. It is our life energy. Energy is always working inside of us, always in motion. That's why our heart beats and why we can breathe and do all the things we do. The Japanese have a word for that invisible life energy, the word is *Hado*."

"That's right, Janine," Aunt Donna answered. "Just as a mirror reflects what we look like back to us, our thoughts and words are reflected back to our life energy, our *Hado*. Our good thoughts and words make our *Hado* strong and happy, attracting good things to us. Meanwhile, our negative thoughts and words can make us feel weak and sad."

"When I first saw my bear, I could feel his happy energy, and I felt happy. So I will call him Hado Bear!" Janine announced.

Janine kissed the top of Hado Bear's head and cradled him in her arms. "From now on, when I see Hado Bear I will remember to have happy thoughts and say good words."

Hado Bear listened to everything Janine said. He realized that when he did not think he was good enough for someone to buy him, he was sad and didn't feel good. But when Donna came into the store and said she loved him, Hado Bear felt light and joyful. Then he understood how important it was to say positive things and have good thoughts so that he would feel happy. "I like my new name," Hado Bear thought to himself.

Janine said goodnight to her aunt and uncle and brought Hado Bear upstairs to her room. She lovingly placed him on her bed. "Good night, Hado Bear."

"Good night," Hado Bear whispered as Janine climbed into bed. That night Hado Bear dreamt of all the fun things he would do with Janine.

When Hado Bear woke up the next morning, he heard Janine crying. "Oh, no!" thought Hado Bear. He wanted to do something to help her, but how could he find out what was wrong?

He knew he couldn't keep his secret any longer. Hado Bear took a deep breath and bravely asked out loud, "Janine, why are you crying?"

Janine was startled. She looked around the room but didn't see anyone else. "Who said that?"

"Oh, Janine, it was me, Hado Bear!" he exclaimed. "I can talk!"

Janine was astonished. "You can talk? I never heard of a stuffed bear that could talk!"

"Yes, I can talk! But why are you crying?" he asked again.

"I don't want to go to my new school today. I don't think anyone likes me," Janine replied, tears running down her cheeks. "I feel different from all the other kids."

As Janine hugged Hado Bear, he told her how he felt at the gift shop. He thought no one would love him and he was afraid no one would buy him. "Then your Aunt Donna said she loved me and I started to think that I was okay," Hado Bear explained to Janine.

"You're okay, too! Don't cry! I understand how you feel. I am different from all the other toy animals. I've always been able to talk. Until now, I was afraid to tell anyone, but I knew I could tell you and you would still love me."

"Of course I still love you, Hado Bear!" said Janine. "Maybe we should talk to Aunt Donna about all of this," Janine suggested.

"Oh, I don't know," said Hado Bear. "She's a grown-up. Will she understand how we feel?"

Janine told Hado Bear that Aunt Donna was very wise. "She told me about *Hado*!" Janine reminded him. Finally Hado Bear agreed.

Janine set Hado Bear on a kitchen chair during breakfast. Janine and Hado Bear looked at each other, wondering when to tell Hado Bear's secret.

When they were almost finished eating, Janine told Aunt Donna that she was crying that morning because she thought no one liked her at school. Then Hado Bear told her not to cry and comforted her.

Confused, Aunt Donna said, "Janine, Hado Bear can't talk, he's a stuffed animal! Why would you say that?"

"Um, yes, actually I *can* talk," said Hado Bear out loud. Aunt Donna dropped her fork and spilled her coffee. Uncle Bill gasped. They looked at Hado Bear with disbelief and amazement.

Once Aunt Donna and Uncle Bill got over the shock, Hado Bear added, "I know Janine still loves me even though I am different. But I'm not sure how other people will feel about me when they hear me talk."

"There is something different and special about each one of us. We are all perfect just the way we are," explained Aunt Donna.

"Hado Bear, I knew there was something different about you when I first saw you, but I couldn't figure out what it was. It's wonderful that you are a talking bear! Don't ever be afraid to show who you are or think you have to change to have someone love you!

"Janine, be kind and a good friend to your classmates. As they get to know you, they will want to be your friend, too. And remember *Hado*! Good thoughts attract good feelings and good things. Hado Bear will remind you, Janine."

YES!

Janine hugged her aunt. "I'll get dressed and go to school after all. Hado Bear, do you want to come with me?"

"Oh, yes, I'd love to go to school with you!" replied Hado Bear, his heart beating with excitement.

As Janine walked into the school yard with Hado Bear in her arms, Janine saw a little boy sitting by himself looking sad. She remembered what Aunt Donna told her, "Be kind and a good friend to your classmates."

"Hi," Janine said to the boy. "I'm Janine and this is Hado Bear. What's your name?"

"I'm Joey," he replied. "This is my first day here. I tried playing a game with the other kids but I can't run as fast as they do, so I came over here to just watch. They probably won't like me. Thanks for coming over to talk to me."

"This is my first day here too," said Hado Bear.

Joey looked at Hado Bear, his eyes wide with wonder. "Huh? Did I just hear the bear talk to me?"

"Yes, you did." Hado Bear said with a laugh. "Janine and I know what it's like to feel alone and different. But this morning Janine and I learned something very important. We are all made to be different and we are all perfect just the way we are. We don't have to be like everyone else. We just have to be ourselves, be kind to others, and keep good thoughts.

"You don't have to change anything to fit in, Joey. So let's be friends!"

Joey's look of sadness was replaced with a big grin and soon more children came over to talk to them.

Janine, Hado Bear and Joey had a great day at school after all. Janine made many new friends. Once the kids got over the surprise of a talking bear, they all accepted Hado Bear and were delighted that he could talk. The other children invited Joey to play another game with them the next day.

Hado Bear told all the children about *Hado*. From that day on, Hado Bear, Janine and all the other children remembered to keep their thoughts and words positive so that they could have good *Hado*.

Take a look in the mirror and see how special you are.

Hado Bear reminds you to have good *Hado* by having good thoughts and saying good words!

Hado
Bear
will see
you
again
soon!

Introducing Hado Bear

Author Kathleen Quigley Caputo has chosen Hado Bear as a delightful and accessible guide to help both children and parents understand that our thoughts, feelings, beliefs and words affect our life energy *(Hado)*, and that they have the power to transform their life experiences.

As Hado Bear often says, "Keeping our thoughts and words positive helps us to feel happy and healthy and attract positive experiences."

In the course of this book, Hado Bear also teaches everyone that, "we are all perfect just the way we are."

For more wise words from Hado Bear, please visit his online home at www.hadobear.com

What is Hado?

Hado (pronounced "Hah-doe") is the Japanese word for the vibrational pattern of life energy from which everything is created. *Hado* is everywhere, in every aspect of nature, and in all living creatures. *Hado* is dynamic, always in motion, always capable of change. It is the basic energy of human consciousness. As human beings, we have the capacity to change our *Hado* – our energy vibration or consciousness – and to guide it with our intention.

Every thought, feeling, belief, and word affects our *Hado*. When they are positive, we create positive energy, actions and results in our lives and in the world. When they are negative, we can also create negative situations for ourselves and others.

The concept of *Hado* dates back thousands of years in Japan. Dr. Masaru Emoto, a Japanese author, researcher and entrepreneur, re-introduced the concept to the modern world in his 1999 best-selling book, *The Hidden Messages in Water*. Kathleen Quigley Caputo studied with Dr. Emoto, and is a Certified Hado Instructor.

LET'S TALK ABOUT THE STORY

This book provides an opportunity for parents and other adults to have a discussion with their children about the fears Hado Bear and Janine face and overcome in this story, and what they learn in the end. Here are some questions you might use to start a discussion.

1. What was the bear's secret and why was he keeping it?

2. What did the bear think he had to do when no one was buying him?

3. Do you think you should change yourself to make someone love you? Why?

4. What did Hado Bear and Janine learn about positive thoughts and words?

5. Give an example of a positive thought or word.

6. Give an example of a negative thought or word.

7. Why did Janine name the bear Hado Bear?

8. Do you think that Hado Bear was brave when he told his secret to Janine?

9. When Janine suggested they talk to Aunt Donna, Hado Bear wasn't sure they should do that because she was an adult and might not understand. Should you be afraid to speak to an adult when you are having a problem?

10. What did Aunt Donna say about being different?

11. What did Aunt Donna tell Janine to do when she goes to school?

12. What did Aunt Donna tell Hado Bear about the fact that he was different from the other toy animals?

13. What did you like best about this book?

14. How can you use the things that Hado Bear and Janine learned in your own life?

TURN IT AROUND!

We can always turn around a negative thought by replacing it with a positive thought. Find the positive thought below that will turn the negative thought into a positive one.

Example:

Negative Thought: # 1. There's never enough time to do it all.

Positive Thought: # 3. I always have plenty of time.

NEGATIVE THOUGHT

1. There's never enough time to do it all.
2. I'll never pass this test.
3. Making friends is hard.
4. I feel different from everyone else.
5. I am scared of the dark.
6. I don't like going to school.
7. I don't get along with that boy/girl.
8. I am afraid to try new things.
9. I know I won't have fun at this party.
10. I am not as smart as the other kids.

POSITIVE THOUGHT

1. I have a good time wherever I am.
2. Trying things I've never done before is fun.
3. I always have plenty of time.
4. I always like to learn new things.
5. I find something good in every person.
6. I easily answer any questions.
7. Friends are easy to make.
8. I do the best I can and know that is enough.
9. We are all meant to be different and that's great.
10. I am always safe.

UNSCRAMBLE THE WORDS FROM THE BOOK

1. ABRE
2. YPAHP
3. ADS
4. JNAENI
5. LATK
6. ROAPL
7. NTEEFIDRF
8. DIKN
9. LIBL
10. NDNOA
11. TFERCEP
12. OJYE

NEED A HINT?

1. Type of animal in the story.
2. How do positive thoughts and words make us feel?
3. How do negative thoughts and words make us feel?
4. The niece's name.
5. What the bear could do (his secret).
6. What type of bear is in the story?
7. The bear was not like all the other toy animals so he was _____.
8. What should you be so that your classmates will want to be your friend?
9. The uncle's name.
10. The aunt's name.
11. The aunt said that we are all _____ just the way we are.
12. Name of the little boy in the school yard.

Kathleen Quigley Caputo is an ordained interfaith minister who focuses on providing positive and life affirming resources to children of all cultures and backgrounds. Following a 30-year career as a business executive, she founded Source of Guidance, Inc., a nonprofit organization dedicated to helping children and families to have happy, healthy and fulfilling lives and to better respond to life's challenges.

Kathleen received her Ministerial Credentials from Emerson Theological Institute. She is a Staff Minister at the Center for Spiritual Living Long Island, and has led more than 100 programs for children. Kathleen has also taught workshops on creativity and guided imagery for the New York City School System, the Fashion Institute of Technology, and City University of New York.

Hado Bear's Secret is the first in a series of books Kathleen is authoring to teach both children and parents that we are all perfect just the way we are. Through the character of Hado Bear, we learn that our thoughts, feelings, beliefs and words have the power to change our life energy (*Hado*) and transform life's challenges into positive experiences for ourselves and those around us.

Melanie Hall has illustrated more than 25 children's books. Her work has been exhibited in the Original Art Show at the Society of Illustrators and is in the collection of the Mazza Museum at the University of Findlay, Ohio.

She has won numerous awards, including the Parent's Choice Award and has been an honor winner of a Sydney Taylor Book Award.

Melanie's illustrations have been published by Simon and Schuster, Scholastic, Houghton Mifflin, Lerner, Jewish Lights, Atheneum, Boyds Mills Press, HarperCollins, and Highlights for Children.

Melanie teaches in the BFA and MFA programs at Marywood University in Scranton, Pennsylvania and gives workshops in children's book illustration at the Highlights Foundation. She lives in the Hudson Valley of New York with her husband, her Maine Coon cat, and two parakeets.

47305822R00027

Made in the USA
Middletown, DE
22 August 2017

Hado Bear's Secret

Meet Hado Bear – outwardly an ordinary stuffed toy polar bear in a gift shop window. But Hado Bear has a secret. A secret he is afraid to tell anyone. He is also sad as days and days go by with no one choosing to take him home.

"What's wrong with me?" sighs Hado Bear. "Why doesn't anyone bring me home?" How many children feel the same way? Worried there is something wrong with them. Feeling they don't fit in because they look different, have different customs, speak differently, or don't know anyone.

Join Hado Bear as he is suddenly chosen by Aunt Donna to brighten the face of her niece, Janine, a little girl who thinks no one likes her at her new school.

Find out how Hado Bear got his name and what it means. See how good thoughts and words attract good feelings and good experiences. Hold your breath as Hado Bear shares his secret with Janine and her family. Smile when Janine and Hado Bear both learn that we are all perfect just the way they are. Cheer when Janine and Hado Bear reach out to befriend another lonely child and share what they have learned.

Words of Praise for Hado Bear's Secret

This uplifting story shares an empowering message with children about their ability to create strong, positive energy by practicing good thoughts and good words. It will nurture their self-esteem, resilience, and compassion for others.
~ Erika Stroh, MA, Educator, Parent, Founder of Parent from the Heart

What a great blessing for the presence of Hado Bear as each of us undertake our personal journey of self-discovery and self-identity with him and his friends. May it reconfirm in you the realization of your inner magnificence as greatly as I was gifted.
~ Reverend Ian Taylor, Senior Minister, Concordia Center for Spiritual Living

Kathleen Caputo has written a delightful must-read story for every child. I agree with Hado Bear: Having good thoughts is the first step to loving yourself and being happy. Bravo!"
~ Vivienne Jurado, Actor & Producer, Founder of Girl Love Yourself Now

A heartwarming story about unconditional love and acceptance. I give Hado Bear a big A+ and can't wait to share this story with my children and students.
~ Lorena T. Clark, M.Ed, Special Education Teacher

Kathleen Quigley Caputo is an ordained interfaith minister who focuses on providing positive and life affirming resources to children of all cultures and backgrounds. Following a 30-year career as a business executive, she founded Source of Guidance, Inc., a nonprofit organization dedicated to helping children and families to have happy, healthy and fulfilling lives and to better respond to life's challenges. Kathleen received her Ministerial Credentials from Emerson Theological Institute. She is a Staff Minister at the Center for Spiritual Living Long Island, and has led more than 100 programs for children. Kathleen has also taught workshops on creativity and guided imagery for the New York City School System, the Fashion Institute of Technology, and City University of New York.

Ages 4+
www.HadoBear.com

ISBN 9780998890609

USA $12.9